The Memory Coat

The Memory Coat

Story by ELVIRA WOODRUFF

Illustrations by MICHAEL DOOLING

SCHOLASTIC PRESS ✦ New York

For Elena

—E.W.

For Dianne Hess

—M.D.

All rights reserved. Published by Scholastic Press, a division of Scholastic Inc., *Publishers since 1920.*
SCHOLASTIC and SCHOLASTIC PRESS and associated logos are trademarks and/or registered trademarks of Scholastic Inc.
An early version of this work first appeared in the November/December 1994 issue of *Storyworks.*

LIBRARY OF CONGRESS CATALOGING-IN-PUBLICATION DATA
Woodruff, Elvira
The memory coat / by Elvira Woodruff; illustrated by Michael Dooling.
p. cm.
Summary: In the early 1900s, two cousins leave their Russian *shtetl* with the rest of their family
to come to America, hopeful that they will all pass the dreaded inspection at Ellis Island.
ISBN 0-590-67717-9
[1. Emigration and immigration—Fiction. 2. Jews—Fiction. 3. Ellis Island Immigration Station
(New York, N.Y.)—Fiction. 4. Cousins—Fiction.] I. Dooling, Michael, ill. II. Title.
PZ7.W8606Ip 1998   [E]—dc20 95-30048   CIP   AC

10 9 8 7   03
Printed in Mexico   49
First edition, March 1999

The text type was set in Adobe Jenson.
Michael Dooling's art was rendered in oil on canvas.
Book design by Kristina Iulo Albertson

Special thanks to Barry Moreno, Ellis Island Immigration Museum, and Marek Web,
Yivo Institute for Jewish Research, for fact-checking the manuscript and art.

Long ago, a young girl named Rachel and her cousin, Grisha, lived with their family in a small town, far away in Russia.

Such a town was called a *shtetl*. It was where many of the Jewish people lived. There they worked as cobblers, blacksmiths, tailors, and shopkeepers.

Their little wooden houses and shops ran all along the cobblestone streets.

These houses were often filled with large and lively families. Rachel and Grisha had such a family. And oh, what a commotion they made! There always seemed to be a baby crying in the cradle, a cousin tapping at the door, an older sister humming at the stove, a younger sister pleading for something sweet to eat — and always, there was Rachel chattering away. And in the midst of this and that, there was their grandmother, Bubba, covering her ears and shushing them. *"Kibbud av v'em!"* she would say.

But quiet was something Rachel could never be, for she loved to tell stories. And her cousin Grisha loved to draw pictures to go along with them. From the first morning light to the setting of the sun, Rachel and Grisha's stories continued. They were the best of friends. And they shared all of their deepest secrets.

But it had barely been a year ago that Grisha had come to live with Rachel's family. He had been orphaned when he lost his parents in an epidemic. And there were still times when he would run to the alley behind the synagogue where he could be alone to grieve.

At these times, Rachel's mother and grandmother worried about Grisha being outdoors in the cold, with only his threadbare coat to keep him warm. But whenever they offered to make him a new one, Grisha always refused.

"I like my coat the way it is," he would tell them sharply, and he'd race out into the icy wind.

Then Rachel would throw on her own warm, woolen coat and fly out the door to comfort him.

Grisha always found great comfort in their storytelling game. And once they began, the game could last for hours.

One day, Rachel pointed out a mouse that had run under a wagon.

"Such a long tail," Grisha sighed.

"Yes, he's very fine," Rachel agreed. "And look, he's come from the Tsar's palace with a message." Rachel's voice grew low and shivery with excitement as she went on to tell the story of this enchanted mouse. "Go ahead, Grisha, draw it just as I say."

With his mittened fingers curled around a frosted twig, Grisha scratched a dazzling castle in the snow. In its turret, he drew a mouse with a miniature sword in his paw and a tiny smile on his whiskered face.

And so the two spent many a frosty afternoon in the alley behind the synagogue, with Rachel weaving her words for Grisha's swirling figures in the snow.

Meanwhile, from within the temple, their grandfather's chanted prayers were as comforting as a lullaby. Life was simple and bittersweet, and it seemed these times would never end.

Then one day, news spread through the marketplace that the cossacks were coming on powerful horses and waving sharp swords. They were looking to kill anyone who was Jewish. There was great chaos as babies cried, dogs barked, and wagons clattered over cobblestones. People screamed and shouted and ran to hide in their cellars and attics and barns.

From their attic window Rachel and Grisha trembled as the cossacks swept through their town.

"Russia is no longer a safe place for us to live," their grandfather whispered late that night, as the frightened family gathered together.

"We must not wait for our children's blood to color the snow," Rachel's father added. "We must go to America. In America, they will be safe."

So the family set about making plans to leave. They sold most of what they owned to buy their tickets and said good-bye as, one by one, friends and neighbors packed and left. In the days that followed, Rachel's family wondered and worried about the journey they were about to make. They had heard stories about the long, hard ocean voyage and of the dangers along the way.

But the tales that frightened them the most were of those immigrants who had given up so much and traveled so far, only to be turned away at a place called Ellis Island, an inspection station in New York's harbor. There, immigrants were inspected to be sure they were healthy, and had enough money, and could take care of themselves.

"We must make a good impression, so that we'll all be allowed to stay in America," their grandfather told them, as the family gathered around the table for the last time. "If we make one mistake, we could be separated forever."

Everyone shuddered at the thought.

"There will be no mistakes," Rachel's father said.

"Then we'll have to do something about Grisha's coat," Bubba decided. "Look how torn and tattered it's become. If we're to make a good impression, he will have to have a new one. Come, Grisha, let me measure your arms."

"No!" Grisha cried. He grabbed the coat and ran to the attic to hide.

"*Tsk, tsk, tsk*," his aunts and uncles clucked and shook their heads. "What can he see in such an old coat?"

"He sees the inside," Rachel whispered. "It's lined with the beautiful wool from his very own mother's coat. Inside, he can still feel his mama's touch."

"Ah." Their grandfather's sad sigh filled the room, as a fierce wind whistled around the windows. Everyone lowered their eyes, ashamed at having forgotten how Grisha's dear mother had struggled to make him the little coat in the last winter of her life. Not another word was spoken about it, and Bubba took out her basket to mend the coat once more.

Early the next morning, the family packed their few belongings and said good-bye to the only place they'd ever called home. Together, they made the difficult journey — first by wagon, then by train, and finally, by the big ship that crossed the ocean to America.

The rough ocean voyage took fourteen days. To comfort themselves,
Rachel and Grisha played their story game. By the time they reached New
York's harbor, they had left a trail of their stories and drawings stretching
all the way back to Russia.

And so it was that this family made its way to a long line of people, to the place called Ellis Island. And so it was that Grisha's tattered coat made its way with them.

Grisha and Rachel held tight to their grandmother's skirts as they were swept along in the crowd.

As the din of thousands of strange voices echoed through the large hall, they couldn't help wondering and worrying about the inspectors who watched them. *Would they pass the inspections? Would they be sent back to Russia? Would the family be separated forever?*

They waited in one line, then another, then another. To still their fears, Rachel and Grisha continued their game.

"Once there lived a magical bird with golden feathers," Rachel began. Grisha took out a pencil and a piece of paper he'd found and leaned on a plaster pillar as he drew.

As she told her story, Rachel spread her arms and pretended to fly. But she suddenly lost her balance and fell against Grisha. The two tumbled down and knocked over Bubba's basket beside them. Rachel was unhurt, but Grisha scratched his eye on the basket's lid.

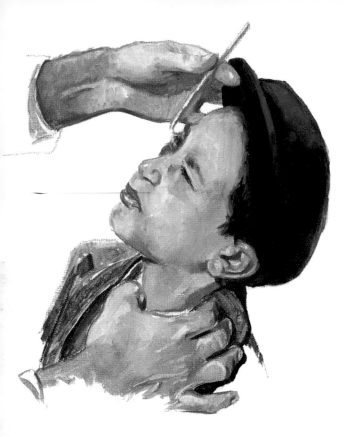

By the time his turn came to be examined, Grisha's injured eye looked quite red and irritated. When the doctor lifted Grisha's eyelid with a buttonhook, Grisha cried out in pain. Taking a quick look, the doctor marked a large letter "E" in chalk on the back of Grisha's coat.

Rachel felt her Bubba's hand tightening around her own as everyone began to talk at once. Something was wrong. Something was happening to Grisha. He hadn't passed the inspection. He was going to be sent back to Russia!

"His eye is healthy — it was just a scratch," Rachel's father pleaded to the inspector. But the interpreter had stepped away. The doctor could not understand Russian or Yiddish, and Rachel's father could not speak a word of English. So the doctor just shook his head, and the chalk "E" remained.

The children were sent to sit on a bench and wait.

"Why won't they let Grisha stay?" Rachel's younger sister asked.

"Maybe it's his raggedy old coat," said another sister. "You should have listened to Bubba and let her make you a new one."

"I won't let them send you back," Rachel whispered to Grisha.

Suddenly, Rachel had an idea. Quickly, she pulled off Grisha's coat and turned it inside out, exposing the beautiful wool from his mother's coat.

Now the dreaded chalk mark was hidden from view, and Rachel's father was able to walk Grisha over to another line where he was examined once more. This doctor was kinder and more patient. And he understood Yiddish. He took a closer look at Grisha's eye and saw it was only a scratch. So he kept his chalk in his pocket and Grisha passed through with the rest of the family!

"Such a one!" Rachel's father cried, as he lifted Rachel and kissed her cheeks. Everyone was laughing and crying at once.

Bubba hugged Rachel and Grisha tight. "You were right, Grisha," Bubba said. "This coat of yours *is* very special. Your mama's touch will be with you for a very long time. Not only here on the outside — but here," she said, tapping Grisha's chest. "On the inside. The most important place of all."

Now, so many winters later, the cousins' whispered stories can be heard no more. But in a land far from the icy Russian winds, Grisha's tattered coat has been passed down to his children and to his grandchildren. And here it remains to tell a bigger story. For in that worn bit of wool, held together by caring stitches, are the memories of a mother's love, and of a family's journey made so long ago.

Author's Note

The first time I visited Ellis Island, I was inspired to write this story. It was there that I learned about the many immigrants who had traveled so far, only to have their destinies determined by an examination. I learned of a young girl who, like Grisha in this story, had a doctor mark the letter "E" on her coat with chalk. This meant "eye trouble," usually the dreaded eye disease trachoma. The child faced being denied entry to America, and perhaps, even being deported back to her homeland. But as with Grisha, luck was on her side. There was a man present who felt compassion for her plight and told her frantic father to simply turn the child's coat inside out!

Also at Ellis Island, I discovered an exhibit of clothing the immigrants wore. There were lace-tatted shawls, embroidered shirts, and wooden shoes. But it was a child's woolen jacket, patched at the elbows and frayed at the collar, that caught my eye. Who was the child who had slipped his arms into those worn sleeves? What had his journey been like? And what were the memories this young immigrant carried deep within his heart, beneath the tattered coat before me?

All of this sparked my imagination, and as I began to do further research, this is the story that emerged.

Historic Notes

LIFE IN RUSSIA

There were nearly five million Jewish people living within Russia's borders during the first half of the nine-teenth century. For them, life was harsh and fraught with danger. During the reign of Tsar Nicholas I, over six hundred anti-Jewish decrees were enacted.

Yiddish and Hebrew books were censored. Jewish schools were shut down, or the students were taxed so heavily that many could not attend them. Jews were excluded from living in certain cities and border towns. Their traditional long coats were banned. Jewish men were commanded to trim their long beards.

Most cruel of all, though, was the conscription, a forced draft of young men into the harsh and demanding Russian army. The length of service was set at twenty-five years for eighteen-year-old males. However, Jewish conscripts could be taken as young as twelve, and many were torn from their families at the ages of nine or ten! Hundreds of these children grew sick and died as they marched into the icy and unrelenting winds of the bitter Russian winters.

By the beginning of the twentieth century, a wave of pogroms (mass killings and burnings) swept through the *shtetls* and *dorfs* (Jewish towns and villages). It became obvious that the Jewish way of life in Russia was in danger of being snuffed out completely. For many, fleeing was the only chance to survive.

THE JOURNEY WESTWARD

For the Russian-Jewish immigrant, America held the dream of freedom and prosperity. Millions packed what belongings they could gather and made the journey west-ward by foot, wagon, train, and ship.

There was no direct route to America. Those coming from western Russia would cross the German border and go on to Berlin and the northern ports. Those coming from Ukraine and southern Russia had to cross the Austro-Hungarian border illegally. From there, they would travel by train to Berlin or Vienna where they regrouped for travel to the main port cities of Antwerp in Belgium; Bremen and Hamburg in Germany; or Rotterdam and Amsterdam in Holland.

Once they finally reached the port city, the journey across the sea proved for many to be the most harrowing part of all. The poorest emigrants traveled in steerage, which meant that they were crammed into the area below deck that contained the boat's steering mechanism. Their conditions were so unsanitary, with overcrowding, poor ventilation, and worm-ridden food, that many immigrants succumbed to disease before they reached their final destination. But the dream of living in freedom and prosperity gave them the will to continue.

Ellis Island

In 1892, Ellis Island was opened as an immigration station in the harbor of New York. Here, arriving immigrants were inspected to see that they were healthy and capable enough to enter the United States. Their names, nationalities, and destinations were recorded by inspectors. When all was determined to be in order, they were given landing cards, which allowed them to enter America. Then they boarded a ferryboat for Manhattan.

At the beginning of the twentieth century, as many as fifteen thousand immigrants could arrive at the doors of Ellis Island in one day! A million or more would come through each year. Every day, the halls were packed with a maze of bodies forming one line after another. A thunderous din of voices speaking in a variety of languages filled the air.

For many immigrants, the experience at Ellis Island was a confusing and frightening ordeal. For Jews, the thought of being sent back to their homelands filled them with terror. These fears were not unfounded, for thousands were detained and eventually sent back. There were a variety of reasons for this, the most common being medical.

If an immigrant didn't pass the medical exams, the doctors would use chalk to mark the back of the immigrant's coat or shirt. As with Grisha's eye exam in the story, the doctor would quickly lift the eyelid with a buttonhook. In those precious moments of the examination, the fate of an immigrant was sealed.

Once an immigrant failed the medical exam, his hopes of obtaining a landing card and entering the United States were dashed. He would be detained and finally deported. This was a heart-wrenching experience for the individuals and families involved. Many had spent their life savings to pay their passage and would have nothing to return to. For Jewish immigrants at the turn of the century, going back to Russia seemed like a death sentence.

Today, Ellis Island is a museum that holds millions of stories and memories of immigrants who came from all over the world — and who now call America their home.